JOSHUA'S KNEES

Juliet May

MINERVA PRESS

LONDON
MONTREUX LOS ANGELES SYDNEY

JOSHUA'S KNEES
Copyright © Juliet May 1997

All Rights Reserved

ISBN 1 86106 211 7

First Published 1997 by
MINERVA PRESS
195 Knightsbridge,
LONDON SW7 1RE

Printed in Great Britain by
BWD Ltd, Northolt, Middlesex

JOSHUA'S KNEES

To the real Joshua, Christian and Arran

Chapter One
"Who Said That?"

Joshua Gray had strange knees. Apart from that he was a very normal and rather nice boy. He was particularly kind and helpful to his younger brothers a good deal of the time. And he was entirely devoted to his parents, who were also rather normal and very nice. Well, his mother was completely normal, or as normal as your usual mother can be. His father was, well – a little different. Very nice, of course, but a little different.

But we'll have more of that later – for now we'll get to the Joshua bit.

Joshua, as we have already said, had two younger brothers, Christian and Arran, and as brothers do, they either had lots of fun together or tried to rip each other's ears off.

Our story really begins when Joshua's very odd knees started up their very odd behaviour. Joshua was ten when it happened. He was running upstairs just as he got home from school to see his mother, who had her head in the airing cupboard.

"I'm home, Mum," (click, click) he called as he jumped up each step).

"I didn't know you had a friend called Dick," said Mum, whose head was still in the airing cupboard.

"What?" said Joshua.

"I beg your pardon!" corrected Mum.

"I said 'what'?" answered the cheeky boy. This could have gone on for some time, but Mum came away from the airing cupboard and they got things straightened out. There was no friend called Dick.

"Well, why did you say there was?" enquired Mum, quite reasonably. Joshua felt things were not going his way, and went back downstairs. Clickety, click.

"Don't speak rudely to me when your back is turned, Joshua, and I don't want you to go and get a stick – the little ones are playing."

By now, Joshua knew he couldn't blame this on the airing cupboard, and feeling a bit worried, as he hadn't, after all, said a word while going downstairs, he turned round and ran up them again. Click, click, click.

"Joshua!"

"Yes, Mum?"

"I said they're playing – you are NOT to play a trick on them."

Joshua knew that old people got a bit funny sometimes – he remembered his Grandpa often gave the wrong answer to questions because he was a bit deaf. In fact, it was hard not to laugh sometimes, especially once when Joshua had asked him, just before his birthday, for a fishing line. Grandpa had gone on for hours about how he was much too young for wine, and it wouldn't be good for him, and what were his parents thinking of, allowing the boy wine, it wouldn't have happened in his day. That was just before he and Stepgran had gone to Scotland to live.

He rather hoped his mum hadn't got to that stage, or at least not quite so suddenly, so none of them had a chance to get used to it. He tried to remember how old she had been at her last birthday. He thought it was thirty-five, and even he knew that shouldn't be old enough to turn funny just while he was out at school. He began to think perhaps he'd better not go the next day, and should keep an eye on her. If he was actually watching, she surely couldn't get old and funny that quickly?

"Why are you looking at me that way?" asked Mum, with narrowed eyes. This could mean trouble.

"I was miles away, Mum," he replied, quite truthfully. "I was thinking about Grandpa. When are they coming down here next?" He hoped a question would divert the way things were going. He walked over to Mum to try and get a close look at her. Click, click. Click, click.

"It's not Easter, Joshua, there are no chickens around – what has come over you?"

This really floored Joshua – in fact, he sat heavily on it in one movement. Click! Click!

"Oh!" cried Mum. "So it was a trick was it? Well, I don't think it was a very funny one for a boy of your age. You are ten, you know, Joshua, it's hardly amusing to start going 'chick! chick!' and expecting me to look round for some. I suppose it's your silly 'Monkey look for nuts' game, is it? Well, Christian and Arran might find it hilarious time after time, but I don't, and I think you're behaving very oddly. Perhaps you'd better have an early night."

Now this was doubly bad. For a start, *Dr Who* was on television later, and he didn't want to miss that. Yes, he had to agree the 'Monkey look for nuts' game wasn't really designed for busy mums. It entailed pointing out some non-existing item or treat, and when the other person looked for it, or better still, held out their hand, you could yell 'Monkey look for nuts' at them and make them feel silly. But why had Mum thought he was doing that to her? And what was all this she kept saying about tricks?

Joshua thought he'd better retreat to his room to think about all this, and perhaps wait for Dad to come home so he could tell him all about it, and see if he had any sort of explanation. Perhaps he had already spoken to Mum on the phone today, and already knew about it. That cheered him – he felt he was a bit young for this sort of problem. Yes, Dad probably already knew, and would understand what to do.

Then he remembered that Granny White lived in a Home, because she was a bit dotty, Mum had said. Joshua didn't want Mum to be taken away to a Home for this particular dottiness – no, he thought he'd keep quiet about the whole thing and hope it would go away.

He turned and walked slowly along the landing to his bedroom. Click, click.

"Joshua!"

"Oh, no," he thought, and stopped.

"You are not to eat lollies just before supper."

"I'm not, Mum."

"Yes you are, I heard you going 'lick, lick'; don't try to pretend – where is it? Hand it over, it's mince tonight, and you have enough trouble eating that as it is, without spoiling your appetite with lollies."

Poor Joshua, another worry to add to his load – mince tonight. It was all too much, and try as he might to avoid it, he started to cry.

Mum rushed up to him, her face full of softness.

"What's going on, sweetheart? Are you being bullied by that horrible Freeman boy? Is that what's making you so rude and nasty to me? I'll speak to the school, he's done it before and I won't have it. No, no, I'll get your father to go and see Mr Freeman, that's the answer, that'll show him…"

Joshua looked up as his mum, glad anyway for the sudden loving hug, but anxious to stop any of the sort of stuff going on she was talking about.

"Actually Mum, I'm okay. It's just that er... I've um... I feel sick." This seemed a splendid solution – not only did it explain his crying, but it might get him out of mince. Wait a minute, though, early bed had already been talked about, "Not terribly sick, just a bit."

"So," said Mum, "THAT'S what you were saying – 'I feel sick', not 'lick, lick'."

"When?"

"When you walked along here, well really you should go to the bathroom and hang your head over the..."

"I don't feel sick any more."

"Jolly good – come downstairs then, the mince is ready."

Chapter Two
The Discovery

Joshua hadn't quite been telling the truth when he said he didn't feel sick. He certainly had a very nasty feeling in his tummy. He really felt ten was much too young to have a mum go funny, and poor Christian and Arran were even younger – Arran was still at playgroup. And what would Dad do without Mum? He seemed to like her an awful lot, nearly as much as Joshua did.

Mum had gone off to get the mince out, so Joshua crept worriedly downstairs and sat waiting at the table, where he was joined by Christian who came home earlier on the school bus. He wasn't allowed to cycle like Joshua because he hadn't taken his cycling proficiency – mainly because he wasn't at all proficient. He seemed happily unaware of Mum's sudden strangeness.

"Noticed anything odd about Mum, Chris?"

"Nothing today, why?" Before Joshua could answer, Mum came in with Arran stuffed under one arm – he was really much too big for this, but Mum always said he was her last baby, and her snookums – and plonked him on his stool.

"I a big boy," announced Arran.

"Yes," agreed Joshua and Christian automatically – they knew only too well how long a discussion on this sort of subject with Arran could go on if they didn't humour him.

Mum came back in with the supper, and started serving it out.

"I'm starving, and I love mince, Mum," said Christian in a revolting display of sucking up to Mum. Joshua wondered what he'd been up to. He was SO obvious, but Mum never seemed to notice.

"Good boy, Christian, I'm glad it's worth cooking for at least one of my sons." Mum always called him Christian, she said it was a beautiful name for a beautiful boy, and Joshua had to admit he did look okay sometimes, with his shiny black hair and naughty smile.

"I a big boy," responded Arran.

"Yes," said Mum, Joshua and Christian.

"Now, while I've got your attention – eat up, Joshua – I've a very serious subject to discuss with you. Only yesterday evening I put a new toilet roll in the bathroom, and it's already empty. Now, who is it? One of you is doing something very silly with toilet paper, and I want to know what."

Joshua thought this was another Sign, and started to swing his legs under the table with worry. Mum was rattling plates, but suddenly looked up at Christian.

"You were sick, sick, sick, Christian? Why didn't you tell me; you shouldn't have gone to school this morning, even if you did want to do that maths test."

At this, Joshua knew for sure that Christian had either done something awful that had not yet been found out, or wanted something badly that he had not yet asked about.

"I never said a word, Mum, I was too busy enjoying my mince," was Christian's sick-making reply.

"Well, who's been sick and used all the paper, then?" demanded Mum. Joshua felt so uneasy he swung his legs harder, and that was how the discovery was made at last.

"What's that weird noise?" asked Christian.

Mum looked accusingly at Arran. Joshua looked accusingly at Christian; he swung his legs again and everybody looked accusingly at him.

Click, click, click, click. Joshua looked accusingly down at his swinging legs. Click, click, click.

It had been him all along.

Chapter Three

When Things Improve

Joshua simply couldn't believe he hadn't noticed it before, but then he'd had a lot on his mind this evening. Suddenly, everything shot into place in Joshua's mind, and he jumped up, ran round the table twice and ended up kissing Mum with a terrific smacker.

This proved to be quite a noisy business altogether, what with Joshua's knees click, click, clicking and the smacker and Mum laughing and looking pleased, and totally, totally normal. Mum wasn't going deaf, or batty – it had been his knees saying all the things she'd misheard. His lovely, lovely knees.

Of course, after Joshua had got over his glee, he started to worry, not unnaturally, about his knees, and what they were up to, and why.

Mum, Christian and Arran all sat round the table, and Joshua either got up and walked around clicking, or sat and swung his legs clicking. The mince was forgotten.

"When did it start?" asked Mum.

"I can't tell you – I only realised it was happening when you all did, but it was obviously with us when I came in from school, 'cos that was when all that business about Dick began."

"Don't remind me, please," said Mum, "I really thought you'd gone potty."

As we said earlier, Joshua was a kind boy, and so he didn't

say anything about what he'd been thinking about his mum, and in fact, he started to wonder how sad she must feel about Granny White being batty.

Joshua did his homework, sitting still, and Christian and Arran had a game chasing each other round and round the table, shouting, "Click! Click! Click!" whenever they caught each other.

Mum was on the phone to her sister, Auntie Rosalind, telling her all about what had happened, and Joshua could hear them both laughing. He wasn't sure he wanted his knees laughed at, but there wasn't much he could do about it just then, and anyway, his Auntie Rosalind knew all about knees because she was a physiotherapist and worked in a hospital.

Just about this time, Dad came in from work, and suddenly Joshua felt really shy about his knees. He put his head down over his English homework, and concentrated hard. Just as he expected, Mum ended her phone call and she and Dad could be heard talking quietly together, as parents do.

His homework had never received such concentration (his teacher said the next week it was his best ever) while he tried not to remember what had come over his knees.

Eventually, of course, Dad came in as Joshua had known he must. He came and sat down beside him and spoke in the voice he used when one of the boys was ill. "Hello, old son, what's up then?"

It seemed so daft just to say, "My knees have begun to click," that for a time Joshua didn't answer. Then, for the second time that day, he realised he was crying again. He somehow felt things were never going to be the same.

Dad put his hand on Joshua's head, just at the back where it began to curve, where he always had done when one of them was upset. And then he just sat there for a while, until Joshua felt much better. He had often wondered if perhaps Dad didn't have a bit of magic in that hand, although, of course, he knew magic wasn't something to be found in your dad.

"Get up, and have a little walk round for me," suggested Dad when things seemed to be better. So Joshua got up, and silently hoped the clicking would have disappeared of its own accord. He walked round the room, not once but twice, just to show his knees he really didn't mind, either way.

"That's amazing!" said Dad. "I've never heard anything like it – it's so LOUD." Suddenly, Joshua began to giggle, and the next minute Dad joined in. Before they knew it, Mum, Christian and Arran had come into the room and started to laugh with them. They went on for what seemed like hours to Joshua, and when it was all just the odd snort, and Mum was wiping her eyes, and Arran said "I a big boy," and they all said "Yes," Joshua felt it really didn't matter at all what sort of noise his knees made.

Chapter Four

When Dad was a Boy

Joshua jumped up, and started going round the room in small jerks, and his knees made a wonderful, Spanish dancing sound, so he did bigger jerks, and his knees were like the best bit of a percussion band, and Dad got a very funny look in his eyes for a moment.

His boyhood had come back to him in a rush, and we need to know about it.

We'll call Dad Andrew for now, because that was, and still is, his name. He was, of course, very nice and also rather kind to his mother, but he wasn't all that normal. No, he had a great talent – he was terribly musical.

When he was Joshua's age, he had battled with a recorder first, in his school music lessons like we all do, but he had got to grips with it. He even managed to make the sounds that came out of the recorder seem to be those which were meant to come out of it, and everyone knows how tricky that is. He understood how to read music, and everyone knows how tricky THAT is. Then, he progressed to the trumpet, and had a wonderful time imagining he was in a brass band.

His music teacher at school had said how talented he was, and wanted to see his parents. Andrew's mother had been delighted. She loved music, and would have been happy sitting

all day every day listening to her gramophone (which is what they had to listen to music on in those days), but Andrew's father had wanted his wife to keep a nice clean, normal house, and have people round for supper. When the music master telephoned, she thought she'd please her husband by asking him round for supper. So she did.

The music master had wanted to talk about Andrew, and how his talent could lead him to fame and riches if only he could be allowed to have extra lessons, and a chance to be in the school orchestra.

Andrew's parents said they would have a long talk about it, and discuss it when the music master came for supper with his wife. They didn't so much have a long talk, as a very short talk, when Andrew's father told his wife that there was not the slightest chance his son would ever be allowed to waste his time in this way. He had to study hard and get loads of good exam results, and go in for a proper life, where men were men and earned enough money to keep a family.

In the end, all this proved rather unfortunate, because the music master and Andrew's mother got on rather well. Rather too well, actually, because this same music master became Andrew's step-father not too much later.

The music master's wife seemed to have rather a lot in common with Andrew's father, because it turned out she had never fancied music much, and had really wanted to spend her days doing housework and having people round to supper.

You can guess what happened – quite soon, in fact not long after the music master had become Andrew's step-father, the music master's wife became his step-mother. They were all really happy then – Andrew's father had someone who loved housework and cooking, and having people to supper, of course, and his mother had a lovely time sitting around listening to the gramophone, with the music master to discuss it all with in tiny detail.

To start with, all went well. After the trumpet Andrew was allowed to learn the clarinet (once his big teeth had come in) in his mother's house, with the help of the music master, whom he now called MM, affectionately. He could practise in the sitting room without anybody yelling at him to be quiet. In fact, MM and Andrew's mother listened with rather rapt expressions, and never got round to cooking supper. He mastered the saxophone, the trombone and even the French horn.

But when he tried to practise in his bedroom in his father's new house (with the music master's old wife) things didn't go so smoothly. His father would leap up the stairs several at a time (Andrew always thought this was to show how vigorous people who didn't like music were) and tell Andrew that he should be doing his homework, and not some wimpish enterprise designed only to sap his strength.

Then, one day, Andrew's father decided in his own rather immediate way that music was no longer to be allowed – in fact it was banned.

Andrew felt that by this time he was too big to cry and yell, but it was certainly what he felt like doing. The school was told he had to concentrate on his work, and his mother and MM were instructed to cease 'encouraging this nonsense once and for all.'

After all that, he felt he might as well work hard, and he did very well. His father was very pleased, and bought Andrew a huge tape deck on which he could listen to 'real boys' music'.

When Andrew got married, he quickly started to be much too busy in his new home – putting up shelves, mending the plumbing, and quite soon, changing nappies and bathing babies – to find the time to get back to music.

And that's why, when it all came back to him that day with Joshua's knees, he started to act in a way none of his family had seen before.

Chapter Five
The Trumpet

Dad (who was Andrew in the last bit) got a very strange feeling in his lips. It was as if he could feel the instruments he used to play so beautifully pressing up against them. The trumpet, the clarinet, the saxophone, and yes! the French horn.

He didn't feel angry with his father for putting a stop to it when he did, after all he had only done what he thought was best for him, but suddenly, DESPERATELY, he wanted to play again. Joshua's clicking knees had triggered some deep-buried longing.

"I'm going to do it!" Dad shouted, and everyone looked surprised because up until then Joshua had been parading his knees in percussion timing.

Dad rushed to the phone and got hold of his old step-father, MM, who had long since retired and spent his time listening to very loud tapes (they'd got a bit more up to date by then).

"Where are all the instruments you used to let me play?" Dad was shouting, because MM was deaf and he was excited.

"There's no need to shout, I'm not deaf you know, and I don't know what's on television today, why don't you look in the paper?"

Luckily, at this moment, Dad's own mother took over, and they had another conversation while important bits were shouted out to MM. It turned out that the instruments had belonged to the school, but he had an old trumpet if it was wanted. If it was wanted! Dad turned to the questioning faces of his family, "I'm going to do it, and so is Joshua! Come on, lad, forget your homework (which was finished anyway, if you remember), we're going over to Grandma's house."

Mum started to mention baths, and school in the morning, and football club, but Joshua and his dad had already zoomed out to the car.

On the way over to Grandma's house, Dad told Joshua the story of his childhood. "Gosh, so that's what caused it all – either loving music or not caring at all about it. What an effect to have on Grandpa and Grandma!"

After a pause, Joshua added, "But what did you mean, Dad, you're going to do it and I'm going to as well?" This had been worrying Joshua a bit, because he didn't know if he cared about music or not – just like the rest of us he hadn't really got round to thinking about it. He knew he wasn't very good at the recorder.

"You'll find out," was all Dad would say, as they pulled up outside the bungalow to which Grandma and MM had retired.

Dad seemed to have developed a strange, urgent way about him, and he hurtled up the drive and nearly knocked over Grandma who had come to let them in. Grabbing hold of her and standing her upright again, Dad said, rather more forcefully than necessary, Joshua thought, "Where's the trumpet, where is it? Has he got it ready yet? Where is he? Can he find it?"

Grandma looked at Joshua, who looked embarrassed. "He's had some good idea, I think, Grandma," was all he could think of to say.

"Well, you look a bit strange, Joshua darling, come in and sit down."

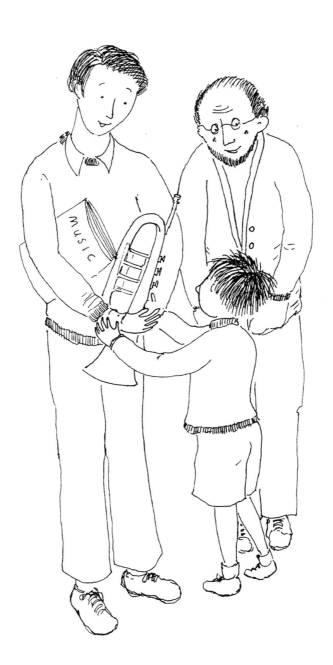

Joshua followed Grandma into the lounge, click, click, while Dad rushed about.

"What's that, you've dropped a brick? Well, you're as bad as your father tonight. Why did you bring a brick in here with you? What have you damaged? Where is it now?"

This was beginning to feel familiar to Joshua, and he decided not to say anything. He eased himself the rest of the way to a chair with his knees completely straight, but it turned out this didn't really help.

"Oh you poor boy, that brick's hurt your legs – wait till I speak to your father, fancy letting you run round with bricks, dropping them and hurting yourself, he ought to know better even if you don't. Andrew! Come back down here I want to speak to you, now."

Joshua realised how funny it was that you were never grown up to your own mum – Dad must be nearly forty, and here was Grandma talking to him just like Mum spoke to Joshua. He smiled.

At this moment Dad came downstairs with the music master, a trumpet and the biggest grin Joshua had ever seen. They looked at each other, and suddenly Joshua saw the small boy that had been his father all those years ago, wanting to play music.

"Terrific, Dad! Let's go home and you can start remembering how to do it." Forgetting himself, Joshua jumped up and ran across the lounge to Dad. Clickety click, clickety click.

"Oh no, Joshua," said Grandma in a shocked voice, "he didn't nick it, it's a present."

Chapter Six
Was There a Cure?

When Joshua lay in bed that night, he thought what an amazing day it had been. Arran was asleep, and Christian was pretending to be because Mum had just been up to say 'Goodnight.' That reminded Joshua of something. "Chris, what're you up to?"

"Nothing."

"You said that far too quickly, you didn't even have time for a 'what do you mean?', so that proves it. You'd better tell me."

Before Joshua could extract anything more from Christian, a haunting sound came up the stairs to their bedroom. Joshua swung half out of his top bunk and looked down at Christian, who had sat up.

"It's the trumpet!"

They both lay down and went off to sleep quicker than they could ever remember.

In the morning, Joshua asked Dad at breakfast how he had got on.

"Joshua, it was like every treat I've ever had, rolled into one. And it's all thanks to your knees."

This, of course, reminded Joshua that he had to face a day at school with his knees behaving oddly. He knew only too well what happened to boys at school when anything at all was out of the ordinary, and this was worse than most.

Just then, Mum came in with the milk. "By the way, Joshua, send your homework in with Christian, because you can't go to school today."

This sounded promising.

"Oh dear, Mum, why not?" Joshua tried not to sound too delighted.

"Don't try to be like Christian, dear, it doesn't sound right on you."

So Mum did notice Christian's sickening behaviour!

"Okay – great! Why not?"

"That's more like it. I'm taking you to see Auntie Rosalind, for her to have a look at your knees. Dad and I agree that we shall have to try and do something about it, for your sake if nothing else."

Joshua thought they had already done a LOT about it by saving his life at school today, but he didn't say so.

After breakfast, Mum gave Christian his school bus money, as it was Friday.

"Goodbye, Mummy, I will miss you at school today," purred Christian. Mum narrowed her eyes, but kissed Christian and gave him a hug, as usual.

"I a big boy," said Arran.

"Yes," said everyone else.

Dad gave Mum a big kiss which made her smile at him, and went off to work whistling, which was really unusual.

Mum picked up Arran, and got him sorted out in his car seat, while Joshua went and got some crisps for the journey. It wasn't actually a very long journey, but he had the funny feeling that today was a bit like a holiday.

After about an hour, they arrived at Auntie Rosalind's house. Friday was her day off, so she was at home. She and

Mum kissed, and both talked at once to each other for a bit, and then Mum had to wake Arran up, and he cried, and then Joshua had to get out of the car and walk up to Auntie Rosalind. Click, click, clickety click, he went. He held his breath – was he curable?

Auntie Rosalind took them all inside, and left Mum with Arran who was now eating crisps instead of crying. She and Joshua went into the lounge, click, click, click, and she asked Joshua to bend, stretch, walk, run and all sorts of other rather trickier things.

When he'd finished, and she'd felt all round his knees (luckily she had warm hands) and waggled them back and forth a bit, Auntie Rosalind called Mum in.

"I can't find a single reason why these knees should be doing this," she said. Joshua didn't like his knees talked about as though they didn't belong to him, and him alone – they might be behaving oddly, but they were his. Still, he was much too kind to be rude to Auntie Rosalind, so he just looked interested.

"Oh dear," said Mum, "I really hoped you were going to be able to put everything right. It's awfully noisy round the house you know, Rosalind."

"Perhaps it will wear off, dear. Now that you're here, I hope you're staying for lunch." So that was that. No wonderful cure for clicking knees, but a jolly nice lunch and no school, after all, so it was still quite a good day.

Chapter Seven
What Christian Had Done

Dad came home from work really early, and said it was Friday, so why not? Straight away he got out his trumpet, and called Joshua to stand beside him. "Now," he said in a businesslike way, "this is jazz I'm going to play, and when you've got the rhythm, I want you to bend and straighten, bend and straighten, in time. Get it?"

Joshua got it, alright, only too plainly. He was going to be the percussion! Actually, once Dad got going properly and Joshua got into the swing of it, they made a really wonderful sound. He could tell Dad was thrilled because his eyes were awfully twinkly despite the hard blowing, and Mum and Arran came in to watch and listen, and Arran never once claimed to be a big boy, he was so busy swinging his short legs to see if they would click (they didn't).

Christian came in from school with a note for Mum, and went straight out of the room. This caused a bit of a halt in the music, and Mum and Dad looked at each other. Joshua thought Mum's eyes narrowed a bit when she was reading the note, but he couldn't be sure, because she jumped up and went after Christian. They heard her call, "Christian..." but then the door shut, rather loudly, Joshua thought. He realised that this must be what Christian had been trying to soften, and got a bit worried for him.

He and Dad played a few more numbers, but the fun had gone out of it, and Joshua soon went to investigate what had become of his brother.

He found Christian with a very red face doing lots of howling and crying, with Mum looking sternly down at him. Dad came in, and Mum turned to say, "It's a note from the school. They say could they please have the last three weeks' bus money, as we're meant to pay weekly."

"Well, you'd better let them have it – that was pretty careless," said trusting old Dad.

"Christian is given the bus money every week to take to school, aren't you, Christian?" Mum sounded very unlike her usual self, and even Joshua felt worried. "You've kept three weeks' money, haven't you, Christian." This didn't sound like a question, more of an answer.

We won't go into the details of the unpleasant scene that followed, because this is a happy story really, but Christian probably won't be doing that again. He said he needed the money for Mum's birthday, which was coming up, because he loved her so much and had spent his pocket money on sweets, when he had meant to save it.

Everyone forgave Christian quite quickly, mainly because he was that sort of boy – he got forgiven all the time!

Dad spent a lot of time on the phone that evening, talking to friends and family, and Mum got her pleased look when a party was in the air.

Just like the night before, the three boys went to sleep listening to Dad, playing, playing, playing.

Chapter Eight
The Party and the Playing

The next day was Saturday, and Joshua and Christian were up early. Arran had gone for a cuddle in bed with Mum – she always wanted her snookums on Saturday, she said.

Dad had been out and got lots of sheets of music, and was madly practising. Joshua joined him for quite a time, until he felt his knees would break. When Mum came down, she left Arran with them and went out to buy loads of party food, and spent the rest of the day cooking, and finding knives and forks and plates and things. Joshua had a nasty feeling about this party, but he kept it to himself. He clicked around the house, keeping Arran happy, playing with Christian and then helping Dad again.

By early evening, Auntie Rosalind and Uncle Gregor had arrived, and Grandma and MM, and lots of other friends.

It was one of those parties that bursts into life, and by the time everyone had had supper, even Joshua was ready for anything.

It was just as well, of course, because Dad hushed everybody up, and got out his music stand, and music, and eldest son.

Christian got his tape recorder ready, and off they went. There was a real hush as everybody realised Dad was playing again, and the marvellous percussion was coming from Joshua's knees! Suddenly, they all started to clap and laugh, and from then on Joshua had the time of his life. He had no idea he had such good rhythm, and when everyone congratulated him and clapped he felt terrific. It was worth the knees, worth everything to help bring so much fun. When he looked up at Mum once, he thought she was crying, but he must have been wrong because she was laughing as well.

Arran went to sleep on the couch, and then so did Christian, and still Joshua and Dad played on.

When he finally clicked up to bed, he didn't think he had ever been so tired and happy. He heard the party going on downstairs, stroked his beautiful knees, and went to sleep.

In the morning, they all slept in. Grandma and MM had stayed the night, so they still had a nice day to look forward to. Joshua eventually got up, and went to the bathroom. The house seemed awfully quiet. He went downstairs to find Mum, and thought he could hear a pin drop. When he opened the fridge to get out the butter, the door seemed to whisper at him, instead of clunking. Clunking! That was it. He looked down at his knees, and took a few steps. Silence. He bent and stretched. Silence. No clicking, no percussion.

And that was that. It never happened again. Joshua couldn't really say he minded, because it had been rather awful for a while. But he took up lessons in percussion at school, and soon mastered the recorder, too. And reading music. And not long after that, he learnt the trumpet. He progressed, as well – you've guessed – to the clarinet (he had his big teeth), the saxophone and even the French horn!

The only trouble Joshua had from HIS dad was trying to get his homework done, instead of always practising music with him.

Christian soon took up the recorder at school (and he never hung on to the bus money again), and Arran, being such a big boy, got a couple of drums to bang on.

I expect they're all playing together while you're reading this.